LITTLE CAT NEEDS
SPACE

WRITTEN
& ILLUSTRATED
BY DORI DURBIN

Know your place when you need space!
Dori

Written for those who are stubborn, independent, and, loving at heart. Use your God-given talents daily to find joy and love others. A very special thank you to those who always believe in me... my amazing and supportive family: Tom, Isaac, and Olivia, and my mama... and very special friends: Heather, Lauren, and the Night Writer's Crew.

FIRST·EDITION
BOOK
·3·2020

Little Cat loves a cozy clean place where
she can relax in the calm quiet.

A place where she slowly stretches
and soaks up the sun.

Where she grooms each whisker and hair.

Where she wraps her tail-tip up tight and
sends purr-rings round her ribs.

USUALLY, this cozy place is easy to find, but today
Little Cat has a problem . . .

Dog.

He wants to be in her space!

The space Little Cat needs . . .

Dog simply doesn't see!

Dog's constant "WOOFS" make Little Cat's tail . . .

Little Cat tries to find space, but every place she tries . . .

on top of the chair,

under the table,

behind the vase,

and between
the pillows . . .

Dog is **still** in her space!

Little Cat
ponders how to
get some space
from Dog.

This plan should get her more space!

But, Dog's nose is too good! Little Cat has Dog hide next.

But, Dog hides too loudly.
This plan isn't working!

Little Cat tries a new plan!

KEEP YOUR
EYES OPEN,
MR. FUZZBY!

Outside she won't need to hide! Little Cat goes in, under, and . . .

to the wide outside! Here she can find a clean and calm space! Little Cat ventures downhill, but . . .

leaves Little Cat muddy and confused.
This isn't really the cleanest place!
She will keep looking!

and rows of cars noisily rocket past.
This certainly isn't the quietest place! She will keep looking!

Little Cat is dirty, feathered, and sad.
In fact, she's never been so miserable.

But then . . .
she hears a familiar sound:

and now she is glad that Dog is loud!
But where, where will she look
for a quiet place?

Little Cat knows exactly where to go next.

Little Cat realizes that SOMETIMES she needs a calm and quiet place.
And OTHER TIMES it's better just to **SHARE** her space!

All About Dori Durbin

Author/Illustrator

Dori Durbin grew up with many cats while living in rural Michigan. She still lives there now with her husband and two teenaged kids. They still have a small army of cats. Currently, Dori teaches children's art classes, is a SilverSneakers fitness instructor, and a personal trainer.

This is her first illustrated and authored children's book. Her cats are planning on many more to come!

"Author and illustrator, Dori Durbin, shared her first book, Little Cat Needs Space. Students immediately fell in love with Little Cat, Dog, and Mr. Fuzzby. This beautifully illustrated and well-written children's book will leave you giggling, learning a valuable lesson, and wanting to hear more of Little Cat's adventures. Each page is filled with vivid details, masterful illustrations, and hidden treasures. If you have a little one who loves animals and adventure, you won't regret buying this!" — Heather Hartwig, Lenawee Christian Schools Director of Literacy and STEM

"Little Cat Needs Space is a wonderful introduction to author and illustrator Dori Durbin. Little Cat, Dog, and Mr. Fuzzby engage readers with their fun antics while learning what it means to be a friend. Children everywhere will be enticed by the purity of Durbin's illustrations while relating to the complex emotions of friendship captured in this future favorite. Social emotional learning in the context of animal fun will hit the mark for parents, teachers, and children everywhere." —Sharon Eagen, Educational Therapist and Cognitive Coach at The Cognitive Link

Please visit www.doridurbin.com for future book announcements and activities!

Made in the USA
Monee, IL
03 February 2022

89626111R00021